This book belongs to
my friend:

_____

A NOTE TO PARENTS

Abstract concepts such as time and its passing are important for children to learn but can be confusing for them to grasp. Such concepts are also not easy to explain. In *Blue's Dinosaur Week Countdown*, Blue and her friends master concrete information—the order of the days of the week—and simultaneously apply that new knowledge to the more complicated idea of measuring time. This story is a helpful tool and a good starting point for introducing children to the intangible concept of time passing.

While reading the story, pause frequently to review the new ideas being introduced. For instance, the sequence of the days of the week and the fact that a week is seven days might be new information for your child. Reinforce the names and order of the days of the week by encouraging your child to repeat them on every page. Also have him count down the days until Friday and guess what the week's surprise is.

After reading the story, buy or make your own blank calendar. Let your child decorate each month. Make sure to mark special holidays or occasions, and hang it in your child's room. Or make your own dinosaur puzzle. Paint or draw a dinosaur on a piece of flat cardboard or poster board. Cut it into seven interesting shapes, then add a piece each day of the week—just like Blue and her friends!

Learning Fundamental: **123** math

For more parent and kid-friendly activities, go to www.nickjr.com.

Blue's Dinosaur Week Countdown

Published by Scholastic Inc., 90 Old Sherman Turnpike, Danbury, CT 06816

SCHOLASTIC and associated logos are trademarks and/or registered trademarks of Scholastic Inc.

ISBN 0-7172-6639-7

Printed in the U.S.A.

First Scholastic Printing, July 2003

Blue's Dinosaur Week Countdown

by
Tod Olson

illustrated by
Karen Craig

SCHOLASTIC INC.

New York   Toronto   London   Auckland   Sydney
Mexico City   New Delhi   Hong Kong   Buenos Aires

One Friday afternoon Miss Marigold gathered Blue and her classmates together. "Next week is Dinosaur Week. Every day we'll do dinosaur activities. And next Friday, there will be a big surprise."

"Hooray!" everyone shouted.

Sunday
Monday
Tuesday
Wednesday
Thursday
Friday
Saturday
1 2 3 4 5 6
7 8 9 10 11 12 13
14 15 16 17 18 19 20
21 22 23 24 25 26 27
28 29 30 31

On the way out, Blue and her friends were bursting with excitement.

"I love dinosaurs!" cried Periwinkle. "I can't wait for Dinosaur Week!"

"I wonder what the surprise will be," Magenta said. "I hope it's something big and colorful."

"I can't wait to find out," Green Puppy added. "How long is it until next Friday?"

Blue thought for a minute. "I don't know," she said. "A long time, I think."

At home, Blue told everyone about Dinosaur Week. "And then on Friday, there's going to be a big surprise!" she finished. "Is Friday a long time away?"

"Next Friday is one week away," Mr. Salt said.

"But how long is that?" Blue asked.

"Let's look at the calendar," Mrs. Pepper suggested. "It might help you answer your question."

"Great idea!" shouted Blue, running over to the calendar with Tickety. "Let's see, I know each box is one day," Blue murmured.

"And all the boxes in a row make one week," Tickety chimed in.

"So how many days are in a week?" Blue wondered.

"Seven!" Blue and Tickety shouted together.

"*Oui, oui!*" cheered Mr. Salt. "Tomorrow is Saturday, then there's Sunday, Monday, Tuesday, Wednesday, Thursday, and Friday."

Blue stopped giggling. "That sounds like a long time to wait for the surprise."

"Ah, but there are only two days until Dinosaur Week begins," Mr. Salt offered.

"And if you keep busy," Mrs. Pepper added, "time will go by very quickly."

Sunday	Monday	Tuesday	Wednesday	Thursday	Friday	Saturday
	X 1	X 2	X 3	X 4	X 5	
7	8	9	10	11	12	13
14	15	16	17	18	19	20
21	22	23	24	25	26	27
28	29	30	31			

The next morning, Blue thought about what Mrs. Pepper had said. "I'll have to keep busy to make Friday come quickly," she thought.

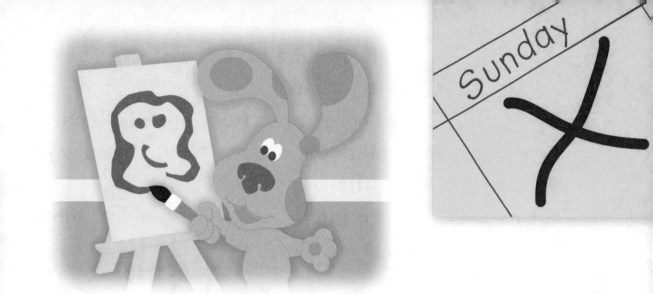

And that is exactly what she did. All day Saturday and all day Sunday she played and played. Before she knew it . . .

. . . it was the first day of Dinosaur Week.

"Welcome back from the weekend!" Miss Marigold called. "Who knows what day of the week it is?"

Green Puppy raised her hand. "I think today is Monday."

"You're right, Green Puppy," Miss Marigold said, "so you can put a dinosaur sticker on the calendar for today." Green Puppy beamed and placed the sticker on the calendar.

During Circle Time, Miss Marigold asked, "Who knows how many days there are in a week?"

"Oh, I do!" Blue piped up. "A week has seven days."

Then Miss Marigold showed the class a puzzle.

"This puzzle has seven pieces, one piece for each day of the week," she explained. "Every day, we'll add another piece, and when the puzzle is finished, it will be time for the Friday surprise."

"Now, counting the weekend," Miss Marigold continued, "how many puzzle pieces do we need to place in the puzzle today?"

"I know," Purple Kangaroo volunteered. He carefully put three pieces in the puzzle.

"Great job!" Miss Marigold said. "One piece for Saturday, one for Sunday, and one for today, Monday."

Green Puppy turned to Blue and whispered, "There are a lot of pieces left until Friday."

Tuesday

The next morning Blue woke up wondering if it was Friday. She repeated the days of the week. "Saturday, Sunday, Monday, then today," she said aloud. "It's not Friday yet."

At school, when Miss Marigold asked the class what day it was, Blue knew the answer right away.

"Today is Tuesday," Blue said proudly when Miss Marigold called on her.

"You're right," Miss Marigold smiled. Then she let Blue place a dinosaur sticker on the calendar and fit another piece in the puzzle.

At Art Time, Blue and Green Puppy made dinosaur footprints in clay.

"I wish today was Friday," Green Puppy said.

"It's almost Friday," Blue said, pointing to the calendar. "Only three more days."

"Three?" Green Puppy asked. "I'm not sure I can wait that long."

Just then Magenta called out, "Look! I made a big Apatosaurus."

They all laughed and roared their best dinosaur roars. Before long, Green Puppy forgot all about waiting for Friday.

Sunday	Monday	Tuesday	Wednesday	Thursday	Friday	Saturday
	X 1	X 2	X 3	X 4	X 5	X 6
X 7	8	9	10	11	12	13
14	15	16	17	18	19	20
21	22	23	24	25	26	27
28	29	30	31			

On Wednesday during Story Time, Miss Marigold read a book about dinosaurs. When she was done, Periwinkle asked, "Is the Friday surprise tomorrow?"

"No," Miss Marigold replied. "Tomorrow is Thursday, then Friday is the next day. So, the surprise will be here in two more days."

Wednesday

"That still seems a long way away," Periwinkle sighed.

"Not if you keep busy," Miss Marigold told him.

That gave Periwinkle a great idea.

"Hey," he told his friends excitedly, "let's all play dinosaurs after school."

All afternoon Blue and her friends played dinosaurs in her backyard. They hid behind trees and chased each other here and there. They had such a great time that before they knew it . . .

. . . it was Thursday. And Thursday was packed with things to do. At Music Time, the class sang songs about dinosaurs. At Snack Time, Miss Marigold gave everyone dinosaur-shaped cookies.

Then they all put on a dinosaur play. The day went by so fast that nobody had time to think about Friday . . .

. . . until they got to school the next day.

It was Magenta's turn to do the puzzle. "Look!" she shouted, jumping up and down. "That was the last piece—it's a Tyrannosaurus rex."

"It must be Friday!" Blue cried.

"That's right," Miss Marigold said, "and that means it's time for the surprise. We're going to a dinosaur museum."

"Hooray!" everyone cheered.

"Dinosaurs lived 65 million years ago," Miss Marigold said when they got to the museum.

"Blue," whispered Green Puppy, "how long is 65 million years?"

"I don't know," Blue said. "But a week isn't long at all when there's so much to do!"